Dear Scarlett,
It's party time! Enjoy your special day to shine!

Sarah Ghulin & Sunil Khilpa

"Good night, my darlings," Mommy said
to Jack and Maddie, tucked in bed.
"Double fun is on the way.
Tomorrow is a special day."

"Our birthday!" Jack and Maddie cheered.
"We celebrate it *once a year!*"
Mommy beamed. "Tonight I'll bake
your favorite fudgy chocolate cake."

"We'll open gifts our friends will bring
and blow out candles while they sing.
It's party time! We're so excited!"
Daddy asked, "Am I invited?"

They laughed at Daddy's silly joke.
Then, smiling softly, Mommy spoke
as she and Daddy hugged the twins:
"Sweet dreams until the fun begins!"

"Touch your nose and make a wish
for gifts and cake on a golden dish.
Wiggle your toes and close your eyes.
You'll wake to find a big surprise!"

They wished and wiggled and fell asleep,
counting birthday party sheep.
That night a singing silver beam
tickled Jack's toes and Maddie's dreams.

Happy Birthday Jack & Maddie!

They woke to find balloons, confetti,
and streamers draped like crepe spaghetti!
"Jack!" yelled Maddie. "Look! That must
be magic birthday sparkle dust!"

It twinkled on their beds and floor,
and on the sign hung by the door:
HAPPY BIRTHDAY JACK & MADDIE!
They ran downstairs. "Mommy! Daddy!"

"We can't believe it! You were right!
Magic happened in the night!"
Mommy gasped and Dad jumped up—
and nearly dropped his coffee cup!

They raced upstairs. The happy twins
bounced on their beds with gleeful grins.
"*See!* Someone started the celebration.
Our bedroom's *filled* with decorations!"

Mommy chuckled. "I think I know
who made your bedroom glitter and glow—
the Birthday Fairy! Have a seat.
I'll share my story; it's really neat!"

"My darlings, I was young like you
when magic happened to me, too!
A singing fairy tickled my dreams
and brought my wishes on silver beams."

"For on *her* birthday, long ago,
that little fairy longed to know,
'Will mine be magic? Filled with cheer?
My birthday comes just once a year.'

'Will they remember, my friends and teachers?
We fairies are such *busy* creatures,
spreading happiness and joy
to every lucky girl and boy.'"

"The day flew by; she did her part
with drooping wings and heavy heart.
She headed home, never meeting
a single 'Happy Birthday' greeting."

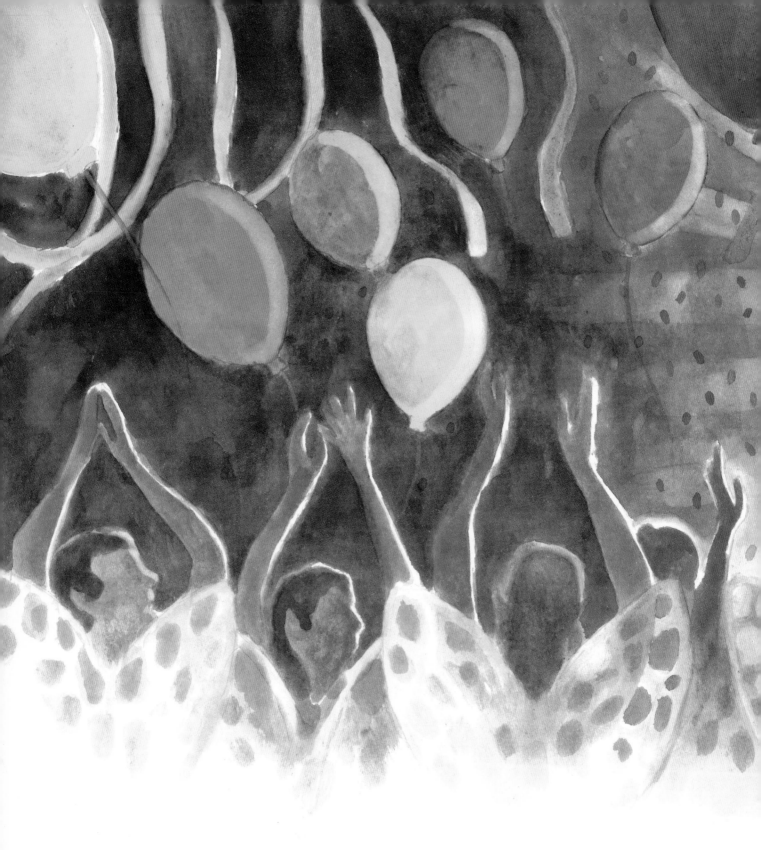

"She wiped a tear and opened the door
to find streamers, balloons, confetti, and more!
'Happy Birthday!' friends shouted with cheer,
for birthday magic comes once a year."

"They *did* remember! She felt blessed;
a wish come true is truly the best.
So she decided, which I find clever,
to be the Birthday Fairy *forever*."

"She guards your birthday wishes with love
and turns them all into stars above,
'til silver beams through windows climb
and once again you hear her rhyme:"

*"'Touch your nose and make a wish
for gifts and cake on a golden dish.
Wiggle your toes and close your eyes.
You'll wake to find a big surprise!'"*

Jack and Maddie smiled and clapped.
Their mystery visit was unwrapped
in Mommy's words, so light and airy—
a present from the Birthday Fairy!

So was it magic? Filled with cheer?
YES!
Your birthday is *special*—once a year!
Happy Birthday!

Happy Birthday to you!
This book belongs to:

_____

(Child's Name)

LINDA KILPONEN grew up wearing party hats and eating homemade cupcakes with lots of sprinkles and icing for breakfast on her birthday. A former Radio City Rockette, she is a dance educator and an off-ice synchronized skating coach. She loves celebrating Birthday Fairy-style, with lots of confetti, at home with her husband, son, and daughter in Morris County, New Jersey. She can't decide between red velvet and vanilla as her favorite birthday cake.

SARAH GULBIN loves the magic of her birthday! She remembers waking up to find that the Birthday Fairy had decorated her room, or those of her five brothers and sisters, on each person's special day— even when she was a college student at Rutgers. Sarah has taught dance and worked in preschools for many years. She lives in Somerset County, New Jersey. Her favorite birthday cake is ice cream cake with a cookie-crunch center.

Interior Image Credit: Dash Peterson

This is a work of fiction. All of the characters, names, incidents, organizations, and dialogue in this novel are either the products of the author's imagination or are used fictitiously.

Archway Publishing books may be ordered through booksellers or by contacting:

Archway Publishing
1663 Liberty Drive
Bloomington, IN 47403
www.archwaypublishing.com
1 (888) 242-5904

ISBN: 978-1-4808-6036-0 (sc)
ISBN: 978-1-4808-6014-8 (hc)
ISBN: 978-1-4808-6037-7 (e)

Library of Congress Control Number: 2018904791

Printed in China.

Archway Publishing rev. date: 06/06/2018